# THE SECRETS OF
# CATSPRADDLE VILLAGE

CALLIE BROWNING

# ALSO AVAILABLE

## Paradise Scandal Series

The Girl with the Hazel Eyes

The Vanishing Girls

## Collaborative Works

Midnight Hour

Follow Callie Browning @BajanCallie on:
Instagram
Twitter
Facebook
**Scan** to unlock the latest information on releases and behind-the-scenes details.

www.calliebrowning.com

*These award-winning stories are all heavily steeped in Bajan culture. I can see, hear and feel my people in these pages and for that reason, I dedicate this book to the ultimate muse: my country, Barbados.*

# TRIGGER WARNINGS

Murder.
Misogynistic language.
Blood.

# 1

## THE LIFE AND TIMES OF ARTEMIS BRIGGS

Per capita, my village has a higher than average rate of drama among its residents than anywhere else on the island. It's hard to believe, I admit. If you were to spend even a few minutes strolling through the wily jumble of brightly painted chattel houses shadowed by heavily laden tamarind and mango trees, you'd be immediately struck by its idyllic tranquillity. You'd marvel at how well-behaved the children are as they play in the road. How peaceful even stray dogs seem as they yawn while the midday sun glares at them.

But I've been living here long enough to know that very little in Catspraddle Village is as it seems. There's nothing particularly noteworthy about it if I'm honest. It's not close to a town nor a beach, neither is it home to any exciting landmarks. It's hemmed in on one side by a quarry and on the other side by big fields that once yielded cotton, eddoes and peanuts. These days they're covered with overgrown grasses that whisper in the wind.

My reputation is that of a man who never raises his voice nor says a harsh word, a deferential soul who can be counted on for sage counsel. But those who knew me as I once was are long gone. Now, the uninitiated see a version of myself that is hard-worn by mistakes and regret. They think I'm quiet and withdrawn when really I'm tired of disingenuous people and the alleged complexities that make them act like pigs. Never once do I reference the events that made me this way. I don't fool myself that I'm evolved. Rather, I'm so ashamed of my past that even the thought of it always threatens to make a bit of vomit rush through the few teeth I have left.

I've seen much from this vantage point. I was born on the day that the Empire Theatre opened in 1922 and I'd like to think that's why I was always such a fan of the pictures. I feel like I've been watching a movie over the past seventy years. I've witnessed the landscape change gradually as the green fields were eaten up by what looked like small microbial dots that were actually houses. Then the poles went up all around with masses of ugly black wires dangling from them so we could lick our mouths with a neighbour two houses down while we waste current by leaving lights on. As a boy, those conversations used to happen in the road on the way home from the fields and lamps were only lit when people needed to see what they were doing. Perhaps the only change I don't mind is that the Kadooment costumes get smaller and smaller every year.

I've seen all of that partly because I live in a rickety house right on top of the hill. It's not incredibly grand anymore but that's only because a rich white man hasn't stumbled across the triumphant vantage point which my leaky two-room commands. He'd probably buy this and all of the others that look like they're tumbling down the slope in slow motion with their rusting grooves and broken jalousies that hang on by God's grace and nothing more. He might bulldoze the humble homes to make way for some massive boxy structure rendered in sharp angles, gleaming metal and glass. He'd tell himself that he's gotten rid of the eyesores that pockmarked the landscape...*historical* eyesores built by people who were born as chattel to withstand the test of hurricanes and housed generations of people who eked their way out of slavery. All to replace it with another blemish with as much character as an unpainted rock to house him and his wife.

Nothing escapes my keen eyes in this village, especially things that I often wish I didn't see, truth be told. I admit that it's entertaining in some instances but in others, I often worry that the police will trudge up the hill one night to question my black ass for hours instead of letting me mind Marlena's business on Days of Our Lives. Not that Marlena is more interesting than say, the drama that went down a while back with that wannabe gangster and his girlfriend's husband, but I wanna be able to just keep the peace in Catspraddle Village if you know what I mean. I don't need that kind of drama in my life anymore.

I had my share of that kind of living when I was young. I was a restless young man with a thick head of curly hair, a broad chest and an appendage that slaps my outer things when I'm running if I don't adjust myself properly. I didn't want for girlfriends. Trust me, word about that kind of thing tended to get around on its own. In time, the women would blush and cast their eyes downward while the men would scowl but also cast their eyes downward.

It's hard to hide things out here. The houses are so close that our property lines have painfully incestuous relationships, what with Mavis' passionfruit vine snaking its way up Euclid's clothesline and his dog constantly shitting in my crotons. It's not hard to imagine that because of that, boundaries are tremulous things, often imagined more than they are enforced, a reality made incessantly clear by the fact that there's not a single fence to be found anywhere in the village. We are our brother's keeper, it's true, making it easy to raise children when a parent has to work late or being able to borrow low-hanging mangoes without permission. But we're not *truly* brothers so the skeletons we keep in our closets are usually those that we don't want our ever-present, overly-helpful neighbours to know.

## 2

## THE UNSUSPECTING SUSPECT

The Barbadian sun rose earlier than usual that morning, shining brightly and casting warm golden rays of light on the dead man's body. It lay in the middle of a cane field in a prone position, his bloated body stuck in a slough of mud that had dried and cemented his corpse in that obscene way.

As the sun inched its way up in the sky, the peal of a crowing rooster in the tall grass broke the stillness of the otherwise silent morning. A thick cloud of flies began to gather; they floated around the body like a cloud of doom about to settle on its prey. The small white eggs they had laid earlier had hatched and now the tiny maggots emerged from their shells, luxuriating in the warm sunlight and the thick droplets of dew that had formed on the man's body. A foul stench emanated from his corpse, filling the air with its rotting odour.

As he lived, he may have been a relatively handsome man with his slim build and six-foot frame. His now bulging eyes may have been soulful and bright.

Soon, an unsuspecting carpenter — who took a shortcut that morning to avoid missing the bus — stumbled upon his corpse and ran screaming back to the main road to call the police. Ironically, after the carpenter spent the entire morning making a police statement, he was still late for work.

Police Inspector Harvey Benskin stooped next to the body and peered into its vacant eyes, wrinkling his nose as he did; he had never gotten used to the smell of blood or death. The dead man didn't look familiar, he thought gravely. In a small society like Barbados, there was always a chance that you might know the deceased. A trail of blood led from the corpse to the thick clumps of bushes that bordered the barren cane field where other policemen searched the scene.

Inspector Benskin pushed himself up from his crouched position with a gutsy wheeze. He was far too heavy, he thought to himself, and it was starting to show. He couldn't continue like this. Today, he would start making considerable changes to his diet. But baby steps; instead of fried pork with his usual lunch of macaroni pie and rice, he'd have fried chicken. He smiled, pleased with himself at his steady resolve, just as the government pathologist arrived to examine the body.

"Dr Best, how ya?"

"Suffering just like everybody else in this blasted heat."

"Yuh ain't lie. So tell me what happen wid this fella here," Benskin said as he gestured toward the body.

Dr Best, a frail little man with light brown skin, a stooped posture and thin wire-framed glasses bent down and peered at the body as he pulled on his latex gloves. He had a very mousy disposition and, as a boy, had been bullied mercilessly due to his small build. His creaky frame was clad, as it always was, in a crisp white shirt and brown slacks and his cracked leather case rested on a square of clear plastic that he always carried for these outdoor investigations.

He looked closely at the small pool of dried blood that had turned a dusty shade of brown in the heat and then at the deep jagged gash on the man's throat. The exposed layers of skin and flesh had attracted some of the tiny maggots. Dr Best brushed one of them aside as he looked at the wound. He scooted around slightly, kicking up a small trail of dust particles as he looked at the deceased man's eyes.

"He's been here maybe since Sunday. The heat of the past few days has advanced decomposition. I'd imagine that he also died right here. The body position is consistent with the pooling of the blood under his neck." Dr Best pointed to a dark brown stain in the mud.

"Murder or suicide?" Benskin asked.

"Highly unusual for someone to cut their own throat like this. Observe the crooked *upward* slant of the slash. And it looks like whoever did it slashed from right to left." Dr Best looked closely at both of the man's hands. "Considering that his right hand is more heavily callused than the left, it may be a safe guess to assume that he's right-handed and would slash from left to right. Also, there are numerous small cuts on both hands, but I wouldn't say they're defensive."

Dr Best went on, "I also believe that he died within a few hours given the amount of blood here."

Benskin let out a wheezy breath as he stooped to take a closer look. "Okay...anything else?"

"I would say that whoever did it will be sporting a cut of their own. I noticed some blood spatter over there that could never belong to this victim based on how far away it is from the body."

"Oh..." Dr Best dug into the corpse's pants pockets. "You probably want this, don't you? He offered the dead man's cell phone to Inspector Benskin.

"Benskin!" one of the investigators shouted. "We got something here." The tall, slim constable, fresh out of the police training school, shooed away a frazzled looking rooster who pecked at him irritably as he fished something out of the tall grass.

The young officer hurried out of the bushes eagerly, a billfold and a small bloody knife blade in his gloved hands. The caked-on blood had glued a short bit of cord to it.

"This is him," the constable said, showing the man's ID card to Inspector Benskin.

"Damian Holder," Benskin mused, studying the man's features.

"And blood pon a box in the grass too."

"Okay," Dr Best said. "I'll have a look at it as soon as I'm finished here."

"Johnson..."

"Yes, sir," the constable replied.

Benskin eyed him shrewdly. Constable Johnson seemed unusually excited about being at a bloody crime scene during his first week on the job. "Search the call records and get this fella information so you could notify the next of kin. And while you're at it, see if he got any enemies."

Two hours later, Inspector Benskin took a short drive with Constable Johnson from the crime scene to the middle of a tightly clustered government housing unit to speak with the deceased's family. The adjoining two-story housing units looked like a row of rainbow-coloured matchboxes stuck together, with each unit painted in various garish colours. Garbage was piled around large metal cans outside each block of apartments. The grassy smell of marijuana rolled with cheap wrappers hung in the air but, as usual, everyone liming outside on the block looked remarkably innocent and not a hand-rolled cigarette was to be seen by Benskin's sharp eyes.

They arrived at block F. The pale yellow unit smack in the middle of the block was perhaps the messiest in the entire neighbourhood. The exterior walls were grimy, the front walk was strewn with weeds that towered over the mossy paving stones and the door had a large shoe-shaped dent in it. Two chickens scratched around in the overgrown front yard.

An unkempt woman with unkempt hair and a short threadbare skirt pulled over her plump breasts answered the door. The skirt did little to hide her wobbly thighs or the sprawling tattoo of a tired-looking leopard perched on the mounds of her breasts. A chest piercing to the left represented the leopard's eyes. It never failed to astonish Benskin that murder victim's relatives almost always looked like this woman.

Professionally and politely, Benskin said, "Good morning, miss. Does a Damian Holder reside at this address?"

"He steal Miss Estwick limes again? That old woman ain't got nothing to do? She always calling 'bout her frowsy limes, but I tell that boy to stop with that foolishness."

She peeped around the men's shoulders, glaring menacingly at a withered old woman who was looking through her upstairs bedroom window. "You could always see when my brother take your limes but why you can't see that your granddaughter steal my man?"

"Uh... ma'am, we're not here about citrus of any sort," interjected Johnson haughtily.

Benskin cast a glance at him and held up a hand before saying, "Miss, pardon, but what's your name?"

"Sherry Holder."

"Miss Holder, we're sorry to tell you, but a man we believe to be your brother has been found and we need someone to come to the morgue and identify the deceased."

Her face fell and she stumbled back into a cracked faux leather chair next to the front door.

Her breath came in shallow gasps and her eyes stared blankly at them before she dissolved into tears.

Benskin held up the cell phone they found in the man's

pockets as well as his ID card. "Do these things belong to your brother?"

Her plaintive wail came with a mournful nod to answer Benskin's question. Benskin said gently, "I'm sorry for your loss, but I want to ask you some questions. When was the last time you saw your brother?"

"Um... Saturday evening. He went by his girlfriend to sleep because we had noise before he left so I didn't looking for he no time soon. He left here with a big box so I figured he would be gone for a while."

"What was the noise about?"

"He owes Stiffy money and he asked me to borrow it so he could repay Stiffy. I tell him to get a job and stop gambling."

The two officers gave each other a significant look.

"Who is Stiffy?" asked Benskin.

"A fella Damian does gamble with," Sherry sniffed sadly. "He lives down the gap at the blue house with the white fence."

"There's a text message that Stiffy sent your brother a few days ago, threatening to hurt him if he didn't get his money."

Surprised, Sherry blew her nose. "You think Stiffy killed my brother?"

"We'll look into it."

Benskin and Johnson thanked Sherry and left.

Five minutes later, they arrived at the modest but tidy blue housing unit. A well-dressed young man with a pressed polo shirt and neat jeans answered the door.

"Good afternoon, we're looking for Stiffy. Is he here?" asked Benskin.

Startled, the young man answered politely, "I'm Stiffy."

"You sure?" asked a stunned Johnson.

Benskin cursed himself silently for bringing Johnson along on this investigation. He made a mental note to tell him to stay quiet for the rest of the day when they got back to the police car.

"What's your real name, son?" Benskin asked.

"Curtis Nelson, sir," was the response.

"When was the last time you saw Damian Holder?" Benskin continued.

Nervously, he shifted his feet. "Saturday night," Stiffy said.

Benskin had been on the police force long enough to know an imitation gangster when he saw one. This boy was no more a hoodlum than Johnson was the King of England.

"Where?"

"By the tamarind tree where we hold the games. I tell him I want my money and he said that I could get it from his girlfriend the next mornin'. Listen, I ain't mean none of the things I tell him," the young man said as he raised his hands defensively. "Damian had me mad last week, but it is only $50 and right now I ain't even want it no more if he sending the police for me."

"What's the girlfriend's name and where does she live?" Benskin asked.

"Her name is Nikita and she lives at a pink house by the corner after you pass the gas station in Long Hill."

"Thanks." Benskin's breast pocket buzzed. He took his cell phone out of his pocket and answered it as he walked towards the police car. "Yeah, doc."

"I checked the other blood spatters I found at the scene and the blood from the knife. One set of blood belongs to the victim, but the other blood spatters aren't human."

Benskin's hair stood up on the nape of his neck. "Where they come from then?"

"A rooster."

"Rooster blood? Hmmm... alright. Thanks, Doc."

Johnson turned to Benskin with a broad grin playing on his face. "The plot chickens."

Benskin didn't get it.

Two hours later, after navigating the rush hour traffic that clogged the roadways leading to Long Hill, the police pulled up to the small pink chattel house where the dead man's girlfriend lived. A frazzled young lady in a neatly pressed skirt and blouse stood wringing her hands just outside the gate, as though she knew they were coming.

"I am Nakita. Sherry call me and tell me that you comin'," she said tearfully as she advanced toward them. "I want you to find whoever it is that kill Damian."

Inside the house, Nakita told them that Damian never made it to her house. He had called but she didn't have any money on her and, in the hopes of repaying Stiffy, Damian said he was going to try his luck at the tamarind tree.

"Stiffy mentioned this same tamarind tree. What kind of games happen there?"

Nakita looked up at them. "All kinds: dominoes, cards, cock-fighting, dice..."

"Wait...cock-fighting?" Benskin interjected.

"Yes. Why?"

Benskin and Johnson exchanged a meaningful look.

"What kind of games did Damian usually get involved in?"

Nakita shrugged. "Mostly cards and dice but he ain't had no luck with nothing so. Honestly, Damian want to be a bad boy but ain't had the stomach for it. He wants to fit in, so he always tries too hard."

Inspector Benskin nodded sagely, an odd look on his face. "Thanks. You've been very helpful."

As the two policemen drove back to the station, Officer Johnson talked ad nauseam about the case, pinning the mantle of guilt on everyone they had interviewed. "I feel it is that Stiffy fella. That clean-cut thing got you trick, but it ain't fooling me.

And the girlfriend? Nah...she too anxious to talk. Feel she could throw us off, but it ain't gonna work pon me."

Benskin smiled lazily, "What about the sister?"

"Yeah, she looks suspicious too," Johnson responded excitedly.

Benskin shook his head. "Alright, young fella, I gine take you back through everything and show you that using your brain instead of your mouth' does get de best results."

Back at his desk, Inspector Benskin asked Johnson to pull up a chair as he spread three crime scene photos across his desk: the corpse, the bushes where the murder weapon and bloody box were found and the trail of blood that connected the two of them.

"You got lots of brains so tell me if you ain't notice anything funny about this crime scene."

Johnson eyed him warily but poured over them nonetheless. Sensing he was beaten, he shook his head slowly.

Benskin grinned. "We found Damian Holder in a big pile of dry mud, almost as hard as cement, which means that when he died it was wet mud. But, you ain't see no other footprints but his."

Ashamed, Johnson glanced at the photos again, nodding when he realised that Benskin was right.

"Now," Benskin said smugly, "you would remember that dis young man was in a hurry to get some money to pay back Stiffy, right?"

"Yeah," Johnson said slowly.

"Good. Yuh also remember that he ain't got no luck gamblin' and that de young boys hold cock-fights at a tamarind tree that ain't far from where we find de body?"

"Uh-huh."

"Good. Here is what I think happened. Damian is desperate for money. He gets up and leaves home wid ah idea to try his hand at something else since he can't play cards nor dice and nobody ain't giving him any. He picks up one of de yard fowls outside Sherry house and heading cross by de tamarind tree to fight this rooster. But before he gets there, he tries to improve his chances by tying blades on the rooster's hock. He ain't know how to handle the bird and by trying to tie on the blades, he ends up with lots of little cuts on his hands."

Benskin pointed at the photo of the bloody blade. "This too small for somebody to try to kill somebody with. The bird keeps fighting, but he finally gets the blade tied to the cock's foot. But before he could get the cock back in the box, the bird flies up again, way too high this time and in Damian's direction. He shifts to avoid the bird, which flies too close to his head. The blade cuts his throat and — boom — he bleeds out right there."

Benskin watched Johnson's face as he realised that Benskin's deduction was the only thing that made sense.

"Honestly, I didn't see that one comin'. You real good at this."

"Stick close to me and talk a little less and you could be good at it too," Benskin said. "I'm going for something to eat. I wanted chicken earlier but this case changed my mind. I know a place we could get some good fried pork from."

## 3

# A BAJAN LOVE STORY

"Tyrone, you hear dat?"

He grumbled and turned his back to her.

"Tyrone," she hissed again. "Get up, somebody outside de house."

"Alright...alright," he mumbled as he scratched his chest sleepily and crawled from beneath the bedsheet.

He blinked slowly as his eyes scanned the darkness trying to adjust to the lack of light as he listened for sounds outside the house. The floorboards creaked beneath his feet as he eased his way to the front door. He held still for a moment and listened again. Crickets raged. Cats meowed as they sifted through the garbage can. He shook his head. Delores was paranoid.

He turned on his heel to head back to bed when he heard a rumbling knock on the side of the house that raised every hair on his body.

"Tyrone, I can hear you walking in there," came a deep voice from the other side of the door.

Tyrone's eyes opened wide. He ran back to the bedroom to rouse Delores, but there was no need. She sat up like a T-square,

her back completely perpendicular to the mattress. "Tyrone..."
she wailed in a whisper. "Dat is Ronald outside."

"Oh shite man, Delores. How he know you hey? You ain't tell
he you went by you mudda?"

"Yes, but..."

The knock sounded again. "I can hear both of you in there."
The deep voice boomed like a megaphone, penetrating the walls
of the small wooden house.

Tyrone pulled on a pair of shorts, took his gun out of the
drawer and headed to the door. He turned on the verandah light,
cracked open the aluminium louvres and peered out. Two dark
penetrating eyes stared back at him.

"Ahhhh!" Tyrone screamed, his voice two octaves higher
than usual. The window slammed shut. He clutched the gun to
his chest to steady his pounding heart. "Cheese on, big man,
you jump me!" He swallowed and wiped his brow. "I cuh help
you?"

"I believe you can help me very well. I came to collect
Delores."

Tyrone cocked his head to a side and pretended to think.
"Delores? I ain't sure who yuh mean. Wha' she look like?"

"Like the woman who just woke you to tell you her husband
is outside."

Tyrone tapped the gun on his temple and exhaled before
opening the louvres again. He glanced out to see a tall slim man
sitting in a folding chair in his verandah. Tyrone racked his
brain; he hadn't left a chair outside.

"Oh Christ, he bring dat with he," Tyrone thought, shaking
his head. Clearly, Ronald meant business.

"Look, big man, I ain't want no trouble. I ain't know nuttin'
bout she being married nor nuttin'. She is just a little catty I
having some fun with."

"Under ordinary circumstances, it would behove me to

inform you that my wife is no 'catty' but given this unusual scenario, immediate reclassification may be necessary."

Tyrone scratched his head with the gun and wrinkled his brow. "Look, I don't like you threatening me. Reclassification ain't necessary. Plus, it sound painful."

The man in the chair simply looked at Tyrone and said, "Tell Delores I wish to have discourse with her." His eyes grew steely. "Now."

Tyrone scrambled back to the bedroom. Delores was fully dressed, her church dress buttoned all the way up to her neck. "You husband is a teacher or something?"

"Wha'? Why you ask me so?"

"Look, just go and talk to the man."

Delores hurried past him and Tyrone put his gun back in the bedroom. Panic rose inside him. He paced for a few seconds, wondering how to get himself out of this conundrum. He heard Delores shouting in the background and Ronald's quiet bass voice countering everything she said. Finally, he knew what to do. He picked up his cell phone, crawled to the bathroom and closed the door quietly. The line rang three times.

"Yeah," said Gully sleepily.

"Gully, it is bare trouble down here tonight. Dis catty husband outside my house all now."

"Tyrone, you serious? Um is 4 o'clock in the morning."

"I know, fam. De man sitting down pon my step real calm. He either mad or got a big ass gun and some men hiding in the bush to back he up."

"Cha den. So... wha' you gine do?"

"Come down hey and back me up. I want you ease round behind he and take he out."

"Dat easy, fam. I going and bathe, cream my skin and get ready now. Wha' time you gine pick me up?"

"Pick you up?" whispered Tyrone furiously. "I tell you de

man got me surrounded and you want me tell he "excuse" to jump in my car to come fuh you?"

"Big man, you know I don't like walking through the dew cause ah my asthma."

"You asthma? You serious? Gully, you asthma?"

"All now talking 'bout this got me stressed out. Getting dew on my head gine only make it worse so you gotta come fuh me."

"Stupse." Tyrone pressed out the call. It was obvious he was in this on his own.

He belly-crawled through the house, peering through each window to see how many men lined the perimeter. They were well camouflaged because he couldn't see a single person outside. Or, Ronald was mad as he had initially suspected.

Tyrone went back to the living room. Delores was hysterical over what she called her husband's 'unwillingness' to trust her, blaming it completely for the breakdown of their marriage. Her husband was calmly explaining to her that he didn't care for this state of affairs; clearly, she and her lover were serious enough to risk her sleeping away from home. Ronald would be the bigger man and walk away from the situation. Tyrone was shocked because if he was honest with himself, he didn't want a serious relationship with this woman. He felt faint when he heard her husband say that he would bring her things over in the morning so she could live with Tyrone.

Tyrone's head started to ache. This was too much.

By now, roosters had started to crow and the rumble of the garbage truck broke the quiet of the night air. The gears crunched and the brakes squealed as the truck came to a halt just up the road. The hydraulic pump huffed and puffed and one of the men shouted "Hold!" as they hopped off the back of the truck.

Delores shouted, "I ain't leaving Tyrone! Furthermore, I want custody of all the children. I bringing them here with me."

Tyrone could hear heavy garbage cans rolling as the men emptied them. He knew it was now or never. The last thing he heard before he jumped over the paling was Delores saying that as soon as the divorce was final, she and Tyrone would marry. Mercifully, the garbage truck stopped right in front of the house. Tyrone jumped on. Ronald looked up and saw Tyrone making his getaway. For the first time that night, a smirk touched his lips. "Delores, your Galahad seems to be deserting you in your hour of need."

Her startled eyes opened wide between the louvres. "Tyrone, come back!" she shouted.

The driver pulled off and the truck rolled away through the dusk. The garbage collector was startled by the sight of this runaway man dressed in nothing but his boxer shorts holding onto the garbage-stained handrails next to him. He looked at Tyrone and laughed as rubbish jounced and splattered Tyrone's bare chest as the truck lolled and bumped its way down the road.

"What going on back there?" he laughed.

Tyrone shook his head bitterly. "You want de truth or a fancy story?"

The collector laughed. "The truth cause the lie might not be as sweet."

Tyrone swatted the flies that buzzed around him as he tried to keep his balance. "De truth is that I need new friends and a new woman."

The collector's eyes widened beneath his bushy eyebrows. "Is yuh friend that got yuh woman?"

Tyrone rolled his eyes. "Honestly, that would be less trouble cause I would still be sleeping."

## 4

## ON THE INSIDE LOOKING OUT

"Good night, ma'am. Does Cody Trotman live here?"

Broken louvres flap open to reveal an old lady who peers at him with her one good eye. The neon cast from the streetlight brushes a harsh pallor on her dark skin against the gloominess of the house's interior. She shuffles around her dentures, making the hairy mole above her lip bob up and down like a buoy on rough seas.

She sniffs and looks up at him. "He ain' hey. Who de body is?"

He clears his throat, wishing that the crickets that chirped around them would speak for him so he wouldn't have to. "I'm a reporter from the Daily News. I'm very sorry for your loss, but I was wondering if...if you have any photos of him you could spare for tomorrow's paper."

She shuffles away from the window and the wooden slats ease themselves shut once again. He stands there, nervously rubbing one foot against the back of his calf to ward off the sandflies that sting him with tiny jabs through his slacks. He hears things being moved around. A heavy thud sounds and a cat inside the house snarls and hisses. Finally, the creaking of the floorboards grows closer and a small photo of a smiling teenager slides through one of the thin spaces between the louvres.

He exhales and picks it up. It's wet. He wipes his fingers on his pants and exhales again. "I just want to say thank you very much and again, I'm sorry for your loss. "Is there anything you want to say about Cody?"

"No, young man. Get home safely."

He walks down the steps. He makes it as far as the glowing circle beneath the pole that soaks his car in neon light and heaves a sigh of relief. He thinks he is free. He is wrong. No sooner than the key swings in the engine, a loud wail shatters the silence of the night. He bites his lip and looks at the tiny photo in his hand. He turns off the engine and makes his way back up the steps.

~

"Part you was? You got me and the whole press room hold up." His editor snatches the photo from his fingertips and waddles quickly down the hallway to the sub-editor's desk.

"I'm sorry, Mr Edwards," he says as he follows along behind him. "His grandmother is having a really hard time and I just…"

Edwards waves his hand impatiently. "All uh them having a hard time. Lemme read 'bout it in the 600 words you gine give me for the front page. Move quick."

He nods slowly and heads to his desk. He does as he was told, painting a bland picture of a twenty year old man gunned down over a game of dice. A grandmother with severe gout who says he was a "good boy" and now cries that the sole breadwinner in the house was gone and no one will look after her. He writes a story that will be forgotten by the time the newspaper is used to wrap fresh fish from the market or line the bottom of a bird cage.

A week later, he is at another scene. She is beautiful and bloodless, her body unpierced by blade or bullet. Behind him, her former lover is led away as he curses her lifeless form. Angry and sweating, his face is flushed after an adrenaline-filled run across two parishes. "I do everything fuh she. Buy de panty she got on and all! You think she had right talking 'bout how we done? We could never done."

The reporter's stomach churns at the sight of her swollen neck. He bites his lip and goes through the routine of talking to her neighbours and friends as snot bubbles from her eight year old daughter's nose. He makes a note of the child's age and name, a footnote at the end of this woman's short life.

In the bullpen, he crafts another good journalistic piece, barren of objectivity, inference, opinions or sympathy. Phones ring, the fax machine whirs and the lady from the traffic department rushes past him with a last minute ad. He stares at the computer and taps his fingers on the desk. The sports journalists are packing up to go to night cricket, hedging bets on which team will win. The writer with the cat photos who runs the advice column is on the phone with her hairdresser gossiping about one of the day's more scandalous letters. "She live out by my sister. I know it is she because how many other women bout hey got a husband who serve in Iraq? No Bajan men don't be in the Yankee army. Girl, he outside woman in the States pregnant and it killing she." She laughs, her belly shaking when she slaps the table. "Read the paper tomorruh and see what I tell she. It gine be a whole movie."

The young man shakes his head. He has always wondered why human beings are so quick to revel in others' suffering and ignore the real issues. He stands and walks the short distance to the editor's office. He knocks and Mr. Edwards tells him to come in. Edwards' chin is filled with sugary crumbs from his jam puff. A blob of mushed strawberries is on his finger. "Yeah."

"I was wondering if you gave some more thought to me doing the weekly column about violence in the Caribbean and the social and financial impact on Barbados."

Edwards rubs his eye and the jam gets lodged in his brow. "I ain't need to give it no thought and I tell you so last time. That kind of thing too depressing. Nobody want to read that. Plus advertisers don't like so much misery. We got to do cutbacks as it is."

The young man rubs one foot against the back of his calf and tries again. "I understand, but people don't think past the drama of the murder to what life is like for the families that are impacted. Children getting passed around by relatives, less income for already struggling families. Do you remember the lady whose son was gunned down last month?"

"Which one?"

"Out by the Careenage."

"Wha' bout she?"

"I saw her last week and when I asked how she was holding up, she was confused. Then she told me how only that morning her son told her to feed the dogs. The same son that died."

Edwards cocks an eyebrow. The blob of jam falls on his white shirt next to another red stain. "Man... she mussy just losing she marbles."

" 'Just losing her marbles'? No, sir. I think she's sick. Her daughter is taking it on, face drawn and small now. The father hasn't been to work since."

Edwards rolls his eyes. "Just forget it, nuh. All now I trying to get another page for the gossip spread because that's what's keeping these doors open. We ain't got the time, money or space for no column 'bout dead people. That is the politician's problem. Close de door when you leave."

At home, the night sky is filled with stars that twinkle at him. His phone never rings and visitors never drop by. On days like this, after standing over dead bodies and hearing victims recount graphic details in court, he thinks back on his life. How different things would be if his father had thought for a moment before snapping his mother's neck. A middling existence in the children's home. Bullying and teasing. Dreams of being a psychiatrist but knowing that the world makes no provisions for those who are average. Only if he was exceptional would he have gotten a scholarship and lived a TV movie life.

He thinks of siblings he could have had, a family divided down the middle with each side blaming the other. A father he hasn't seen in years. Girlfriends who feared he had inherited his father's temper. The lies he told to cover his past, the truths he told that hurt his future. He closes his eyes against the thoughts that swirl around him like dust and the night closes in like an obsidian cloud. He rubs his head and the tears come again. He's grown weary of an empty life. He wonders if there's any good he could ever do. "Be the change you want to see in the world," he mutters. Patting the backs of family members and writing sterile news changes nothing. It drives him deeper into a dark place where hope is suffocating slowly. He takes another swallow of his drink. It's the only thing that helps him sleep. He needs to drink a lot more before the warmth completely envelopes his body and lets his mind rest. Secretly he hopes it will help him sleep forever.

## 5

# THE SCIENCE OF GARBAGE

I does work the stretch from Bridgetown to Brixton, enough of a distance that I get to see some of everything. Not literally *see* since most of my job does happen in the dead of night. But even in the dark, dealing with the garbage the world leaves behind, I become a scientist, an analyst of human behaviour. There ain't much I don't glean from trash, but I doubt you know how much you say to me with what you throw away.

My day does start when the tele-classifieds begin at two o'clock in the morning. Lucky for me, my bedroom at the back by the kitchen so I could get ready without waking my mother. The soft bluish glow from the TV is the only light in the house as I pad down the tiny corridor, my feet sticking to the congoleum and making a sound like suction cups as I walk. My old lady leaves porridge on the table in a red and black Thermos flask that looks like it make from one of those Scottish men kilts. Mumzy was keeping my drinks in that since I was born and as I get older I realize how special it is to have something so constant in my life. Yeah, the flask old-fashioned and no amount of baking soda and vinegar my mother rub on the inside can't get off them yellow stains, but I don't believe in throwing 'way things just because them age a little. Them stains add character.

I fill my enamel cup and drink my oats as I stand by the kitchen sink. I ain't no big breakfast man so oats does do me just fine. After that, I feed Dipper, pat he big slobbery head, bathe and dress in the yard and go through the paling just in time to see Cephus coming up the gap in the Datsun 120Y. And all of this does happen before the roosters could even cock open them two eyes.

Cephus is my man, even though we differ in a lot of ways. We weren't business with books when we was at school, but we ain't block boys rolling blunts under streetlights and calling we-selves soldiers for no drug lord neither. That is a bunch of shite. Block boys get paid with spliffs to do dirty work for rich white men that live in the heights and terraces. Block boys' wages literally go up in smoke 'cause a white man would tell them to take a little kilo for themselves and hand them a bottle of brandy to drink. But block boys never got money to give them child mothers or help pay a bill in the family house. Jackasses. Me and Cephus went to the constituency office straight outta school to ask for work. Them send we down to Sanitation and we was there since then.

We live in a section of the village called The Oaks and every morning by three o'clock we does roll through like secret agents, driving slow with the headlights on dim so nobody don't think we is the police and start shooting at we. Big orange street lamps does light the way through the development like huge fireflies shining their asses on the sidewalk. By the time we pull onto the highway, only a few cars are on the road, so Cephus could open up the 120 and give the gas station limers some handbrake action. One time Cephus gave them a little *too* much action, cut the corner real neat and knock off the muffler. We was shame when we went back for it, but the fellas by the gas station didn't give we too much heat. It's Tuesday morning though, so not a boy at the gas station. Even limers got enough respect for the system to make sure they get to work on time every morning.

By the time we park in Sanitation's yard, our driver, Barry, is already there so we move out the same time. Drivers are the supervisors and from the time we started working at Sanitation, Barry say, "Sooner we leave, the sooner we back home drawing up under we women. Dem fellas picking up garbage in the hot sun gonna be too tired to sex them girls when they get back, but I old so I gotta conserve the little energy I got."

Me and Cephus looked at one another and laughed, telling we-selves that he just saying so to motivate we. Till the day we see this sweet light-skinned girl come to collect Barry and then we understood why we is always the first to leave the yard.

All three of us sit up front in the cab when we leave the yard; no need to hang off the back like sloths until we get to the start of our route. Plus, it's more fun to listen to Barry talk on the way down the road. Barry was collecting garbage for over forty years, so he see a lot and always got a war story to tell. This morning, he talks about the time an outside man was running from his woman's husband and escaped on the garbage truck. Barry say the man hop over a paling, fly over the sidewalk and grab onto the rails next to Barry in nothing but he bare boxers. Barry is in fits and can barely talk with all the tears running down he rummy cheeks. "If you see all the garbage juice splashing up on the man chest. Thing is... we just collected all the nasty chicken innards and the old oil from the fry shop and the man boxers was in a state. I *telling* you he never wear them again."

Man, we laugh at that until we reach Bridgetown. The decorative lanterns that line the empty streets start to flicker and go off as the auto timers kick in. At the top of Broad Street, right in front of the old Mutual Building, me and Cephus get out to start collecting.

We uncover the fancy bins the government set up alongside the road plastered with big signs telling we to stop littering because garbage does run 'way the tourists. Before that, I have to sweep the gutters, gathering up souvenir wrappers and pencils with hand-stitched dolls at the end where the erasers should be. The dolls look like Mother Sallys in traditional dress, dark skin mimicked by brown fabric and black yarn that's meant to be hair. I bet you no locals ain't leave those things there. That is tourist trash, plain and simple. I read once that tourism does contribute some double-digit percentage of pollution to the island. I see British and American people on the beach throwing cigarette butts in the water and leaving bottles on the sand. All those ads on TV telling Bajans that tourism is our business, let's play our part, but I never once see one telling tourists to play theirs.

Inside those bins is mostly run-of-the-mill garbage: soda bottles, Kiss Cake wrappers and that kind of thing. I does hardly see apple cores or banana peels in there, definitely no leftover celery stalks. Probably why the diabetes rate so high and the island is the amputation capital of the world. Maybe the government should put posters on the bins with one-foot people looking miserable in wheelchairs instead of smiling Bajans giving directions to tourists.

The good thing about working with Cephus is that we don't do a lot of talking at work, so we get through quick. I handle the left side of the road, Cephus does the right, and we go like that until the sun starts to peek over the Constitution River, leaving a long strip of light on the water that shines so pretty you'd think gold was beneath the surface. The river marks the end of the commercial garbage we collect. Before long, Barry turns right and drives us out of town.

The roads on the outskirts of town are the worst. It took time to get used to the jouncing at first, the way the truck jiggling up and down on the uneven parts. But after a while, you learn the rhythm of the roads, the coordinates of each pothole and raised sewer grate and your body start to sway even before you get there. Soon, riding the back of the truck is like floating on a cloud. Only a man with a limber body could make hanging off the back of a rubbish truck look so graceful, and I full of grace.

As we round the corner by the traffic lights, another smell start to mix in with the garbage that would make you vomit if you don't stick a menthol inhaler up your nose. Don't get me wrong, we carrying rotting food and a cat somebody knocked down earlier and it ain't smell good, but that stench tells me we're about to go through the Barracks, a low-income tenantry area out by the sewage plant. I hate the phrase *low-income*. Governments use that word to make it seem like these people make just a *little less* than everyone else, but the truth is that these people are straight-up poor. They hoarded shopping bags by the dozens right before the plastic ban because them can't afford to buy no big black trash bags to put their garbage in. So that means collections out here take longer since you got a thousand little small bags to pick up. Small bags that are thrown onto a pile as tall as me and ravaged by cats and dogs every night.

The sun has come up enough to let me see rats running like ants all over the garbage piled up on the corner. Me and Cephus kick them away and grab the bags by the twos and threes so we could finish fast. Every bag rings with a metallic clink: empty cans from corned beef, luncheon meat and sardines banging together like church cymbals at Harvest. Sometimes you see drink crystal packets slip through the knots and fall into the road, the inside of the foil pack stained bright red or purple. Nuff salt and sugar are the norms in places like these. In a few months' time, this same corner going to be full of all kinds of trash. And I mean all kinds: old chairs, ripped up mattresses, big screen TV boxes, old fridges. All stuff that they'll want us to take away in *one* day otherwise they get hot and sweaty and start cussing on the call-in programs about how the government doesn't care about poor people.

"Cephus, how you, sweetie?" That is Darlene, a girl with the hots for Cephus since school. Every Tuesday when we come out this side, she sashays through the alley in a flimsy nightgown, nipples printing out and staring at we like two arrows. I suspect she squeezes them right before she walks through the door, same way she does take off the panty so we could see she ass cheeks clapping underneath that see-through polyester when she suddenly got to run back inside.

"I good, Darlene. You going to the reunion next week?"

She arch she back a little bit *just-in-case* Cephus can't see her headlights on high-beam and coos, "Only if you carrying me."

Cephus start to chuckle like a fool, he eyes glue on to Darlene chest and say, "Man, I going see what happen."

Darlene stupses. "You always saying so. Guh long with you buck teeth woman. I ain't got time for you."

I hear Barry laughing as the compactor start to crush everything we tossed in, flicking bits of refuse and pressing gallons of smelly garbage water onto the road, adding another coat to the old stains which nobody seems to wash down after we leave. Cephus ain't respond, but I know him long enough to know that Darlene's words gonna bother him.

A little further up the gap, we stop in front a small rum shop and we just about to roll the heavy metal cans toward the truck when two men step out of the shadows and put guns to our heads. Out of the corners of my eyes, I see more men lurking, their hands clutching machetes that look lethal even from that distance because of how the early morning light glints on the sharpened blades.

Now you might think this frightens me and Cephus, but the

time for frighten long gone. We say "Morning", unpack some of the garbage on top and leave enough to cover the tightly wrapped black bundles that sit on the bottom of each can. We put them back where they come from, big round spots of flattened mud surrounded by a whole bunch of overgrown grass. The first time these men jump we, I almost pissed myself because I ain't had enough money to stop a robber from killing me out of frustration. Since then I make sure I walk with a little fifty dollar and an old gold chain in my pocket for the thieves. But these men ain't interested in robbing we. Them just safeguarding them stash in case we get greedy, and the garbage is as good a place as any to hide drugs when police raid the neighbourhood.

Once the cans are back in place, the guns are lowered and the men sit back down on overturned milk crates, nod and say "Yeah, brudda" as though putting gun nozzles to we head is the same as a handshake. We hop on the truck and roll out. In a sick way, feeling that little buzz on mornings does pump me up and make me feel like my job exciting, but ain't no way I could ever tell my old lady about this. Mumzy cool and all, but she would come down here and slice up these men fine, fine, fine for doing this shite. For my one part, I say a little drama does keep a man on he toes and help he stay calm under pressure. But I still ain't telling my mother; that is a little *too* much pressure.

We turn onto the highway, one of the best roads on the island. It's so smooth that even when Barry changes the gears, the ride is slicker than okras and cornmeal cou-cou 'cause the truck don't stutter and rattle the way it does on bumpy roads. We pass the big open stretch of beach where early sea bathers taking them time to warm up to that cold ass water. Every morning, I watch them cup their hands together and splash salt water on their skin, trying to trick their bodies and lessen the icy shock of an ocean bathed in moonlight overnight.

The salt air blows across the sand and right past us, carrying away the decaying reek of unwanted and expired things that follow us for most of our day. The five minutes we spend going up the highway is the part I love best. That sweet sea breeze does make me feel like I is a man hanging onto the mizzen mast of my own yacht as I cruise up the Riviera with my wife and children, instead of gripping garbage-stained handrails next to Cephus. My imaginary family would laugh as the wind whips our hair while we plan our next vacation as though the money and time for these things will always be there.

The gears crunch and the truck slows down. When we turn onto Brixton, it is a whole different vibe and all three of us know it. To show you what I mean: one time, a black trash bag opened up and the land tax bill fell out. Cephus' mouth hang open like a trap door when he come and show me this thing.

My eyes get wide and I say, "Cephus, that can't be right. This body paying more *land tax* than we does make in a whole year."

We looked up at the house then, a pale yellow mansion with a three-car garage and a massive balcony just steps away from the white sand beach behind it. Cephus was quiet for the rest of that day, mostly because I think he couldn't wrap he mind around a man paying so much for the privilege to live in a place. Because that's all land tax is; the cost of privilege. Land tax don't put food in a fridge nor gas in the tank nor medicine in the cupboard. Cephus struggles with these things more than me. He can't understand a world where he wants a Benz but can't afford it. He don't see that we does get good pay and the whole day to we-selves. We ain't got bosses who shouting at we to meet quotas and deadlines. We set we own hours and live freer than most. We don't spend half our pay at the gym because lifting those heavy cans does got our arms and back on fleek. Still, none of this stops Cephus from griping and living above his means.

He never got money because that 120Y does drink gas and

always breaking down. Whenever we get to places like Brixton, he does get bitter, sifting through the people garbage and complaining about it. "Not a single plastic bottle...you imagine people so rich they got time to sort garbage?" he stupses as he throws in a single small bag. The homeowners in this area operate different. They eat organic food and recycle and compost. Well...maybe not they themselves. These people got staff to do these things and the only time we see the homeowners is when they wave at we before they check them smart-watches and go jogging on the beach. It is the maids and gardeners, people who look just like us, who come outside with these small bags with barely any garbage which never seems to smell. To be honest, it is from collecting these people rubbish that make me switch up how me and Mumzy does eat. I realize these people always look fresh like dew daisies unlike the people out by the sewage plant who skin always look dusty and dull. Outside of the obvious differences in air quality that come from living next to a sewage plant versus living next to the sea, I tell myself it had something to do with food. So my mother stop buying all of that canned stuff and we does eat more veggies, oats and sago. You know...old-time thing. Since then, Mumzy arthritis improve and I sleeping better at night.

When we get to the end of the road, I spot a little bicycle with streamers that flutter in the wind on top of a metal garbage bin. Barry and Cephus laugh because I collect these things, but I don't care. I put it up front in the cab and go back to hauling the trash. By the time we finish Brixton, it ain't no more than eight o'clock. We climb back in the cab and Barry says, "Perfect timing today. We going get to the dump before everybody and be home before office workers drink them first cup of coffee."

Long lines of cars snake down to town as everyone tries to get to work on time, but the traffic won't let them be great. We going away from town toward the dump in the middle of the island so the road clear. When we get there, me and Barry empty the rear loader while Cephus wipes down the truck. No point in driving a vehicle that always smell sour.

As predicted, on the way home, Cephus leans back in the driver seat drinking a beer and wonders how to get 'way from he woman to carry Darlene to the reunion. All I could do is shake my head.

When we get to my house, I say I'll see him in the morning and to have a good night. Knowing Cephus, he going sleep all day, party until it's time for work, rinse and repeat that pattern every day for the rest of his life.

The house is empty when I step inside. I bathe again then tidy up the kitchen and pack my cart to go to the corner. Barry and Cephus think I is some crazy garbage hoarder like Sanford, but I got my good sense. If I don't find something good on the route, I wait until we off-load and peep around for treasures at the dump. The little pink bicycle from Brixton has purple streamers and a white basket. The chain is off, and one of the fenders is dented but those are easy fixes. That's what I do. I repair fans, umbrellas and all kinda things that people think are no good. Most months I make twice my Sanitation wages selling these things back to the same kind of people who threw them out in the first place. It makes me laugh to watch them marvel at the great deals they get, half of what they'd pay at the big stores in town. I laugh 'cause I found them at the side of the road for nothing. I rummage through the dump for the parts to fix them up and then sell them from a shed on a street corner that I don't have to pay rent for. Since last year I had enough money to open a shop, but Mumzy say not to waste that money. We decide to get a little house in the country instead so we could plant some kitchen garden and that kinda thing. We moving next month.

I ain't on the corner long before a woman pulls up in a fancy Mercedes to look at the same pink bicycle I just finished fixing.

She is walking perfection: nice complexion, tailored outfit, painted nails, not a hair out of place. I watch her touching the bicycle I pulled from the garbage, knowing full well that she would never stop on the side of the road and pick it up herself, even though she wants to keep as much money as possible in her pocket to maintain her image. I learned a long time ago that rich people like to save money more than anybody else. Which makes sense; they can't brag about it if they spend all. She will go away feeling like she has empowered a young man who's down on his luck with her one-off sale. I like that kinda thinking because it benefits me more than it benefits her.

She plays with the streamers on the handle and rings the little bell before she smiles and asks how much.

"$250," I tell she.

She so happy that she pull out the three bills and hand me right there and then. I pocket the money, knowing that not many people make that much in sixty minutes. I put the bicycle in the car trunk and off she goes. As I push my cart home, I chuckle at the irony of life. People quick to throw out things and say them broken, but only men like me who look past the garbage can see the glory.

# BEHIND-THE-SCENES DETAILS

When I first thought about putting together this anthology I immediately realised that I tend to present these stories in small intimate settings that very much remind me of archetypal Bajan lifestyles. Some of the characters could even be people I know given their antics (this is meant *literally* in A Bajan Love Story - lol). That's what prompted me to write 'The Life and Times of Artemis Briggs'. He's a casual observer who lends context to the chaos and drama that takes place in this village, introducing you to these events with a lot of candour and a dash of incredulity.

'The Unsuspecting Suspect' won a NIFCA silver medal and was one of my first awards when I started writing. To be honest, I entered primarily because I felt like I wasn't exercising my writing muscle enough and wanted to get feedback on *something*. I was shocked when they called to say it had been awarded a prize — especially a silver medal. That was my first tiny hint that maybe my writing might be decent.

'A Bajan Love Story' won a NIFCA bronze medal and the NIFCA Special Prize and is sorta kinda based on a true story. Nooo...I wasn't any of the characters in the story but the real-life version is even more of a doozy than the words that have made it onto these pages.

'On the Inside Looking Out' was long-listed for the Brooklyn Caribbean Lit Fest in 2019 and was my first foray into competitions outside of the region. It's the only story in the bunch that doesn't have a humorous side to it and that's because it reflects things that bother me. Not just about Barbadian society but society at large. I'm concerned about how numb we now are to crime. How our governments and the media spend less time trying to find a solution and more time trying to plaster over the issues. Each of us has a duty to help; whether it's mentoring an at-risk youth, voting for responsible policies or holding politicians' feet to the fire about things that impact all of us. Sometimes, it's as simple as venting in a story.

'The Science of Garbage' is the magnum opus of my short story career thus far. I can't begin to explain how much I love this piece. I know I shouldn't choose favourites but 'The Science of Garbage' is definitely the piece of short fiction that makes me feel the warmest and fuzziest on the inside. I literally stopped everything I was doing one night because I could just *feel* the energy of that story pulling me and I'm glad I didn't defer creating that night. The unnamed protagonist is a sharp observer who's so insightful and forward thinking. We learn much more about him through his thoughts than we do through his actions and I think that's such a special thing. 'The Science of Garbage' was one of three finalists in the 2022 Brooklyn Caribbean Lit Fest award and even though it didn't win, I am super proud of it.

# DON'T FORGET TO LEAVE AN AMAZON REVIEW

Hi there,

I hope you enjoyed 'The Secrets of Catspraddle Village', my collection of award-winning and short/long listed short stories. I can actually remember the frame of mind I was in when I wrote each one and that's part of what makes it truly special.

As a self-published author, nothing is more valuable to me than feedback and I hope you'll be kind enough to leave an honest review on Amazon and Goodreads. Leaving feedback helps me to become better at writing and publishing so that I may enhance your reader experience. It also helps other readers make informed decisions about if they may enjoy this book.

Thanks!

X,

Callie

# MUSE MAGAZINE

Visit www.calliebrowning.com to sign up for my literary
magazine, Muse!
(because, seriously, who wants another boring newsletter?)
Free short stories
New books
Sales & promotions
Exclusive Giveaways
Behind-the-scenes photos

# ABOUT THE AUTHOR

Callie Browning was born and raised in Barbados. She is an avid reader and has been writing for public consumption since 2009. She has won awards for her short stories and her books have been featured by Oprah Daily, Yahoo, the Jamaica Gleaner and other. She lives in Barbados with her family.

Follow Callie on Instagram, Facebook and Twitter @BajanCallie

# CREDITS

Special thanks to the National Cultural Foundation for their kind grant that allowed me to produce the audio book edition of this anthology. Your commitment to the arts is appreciated.

Made in the USA
Columbia, SC
27 November 2023

27238416R00036